D1119970

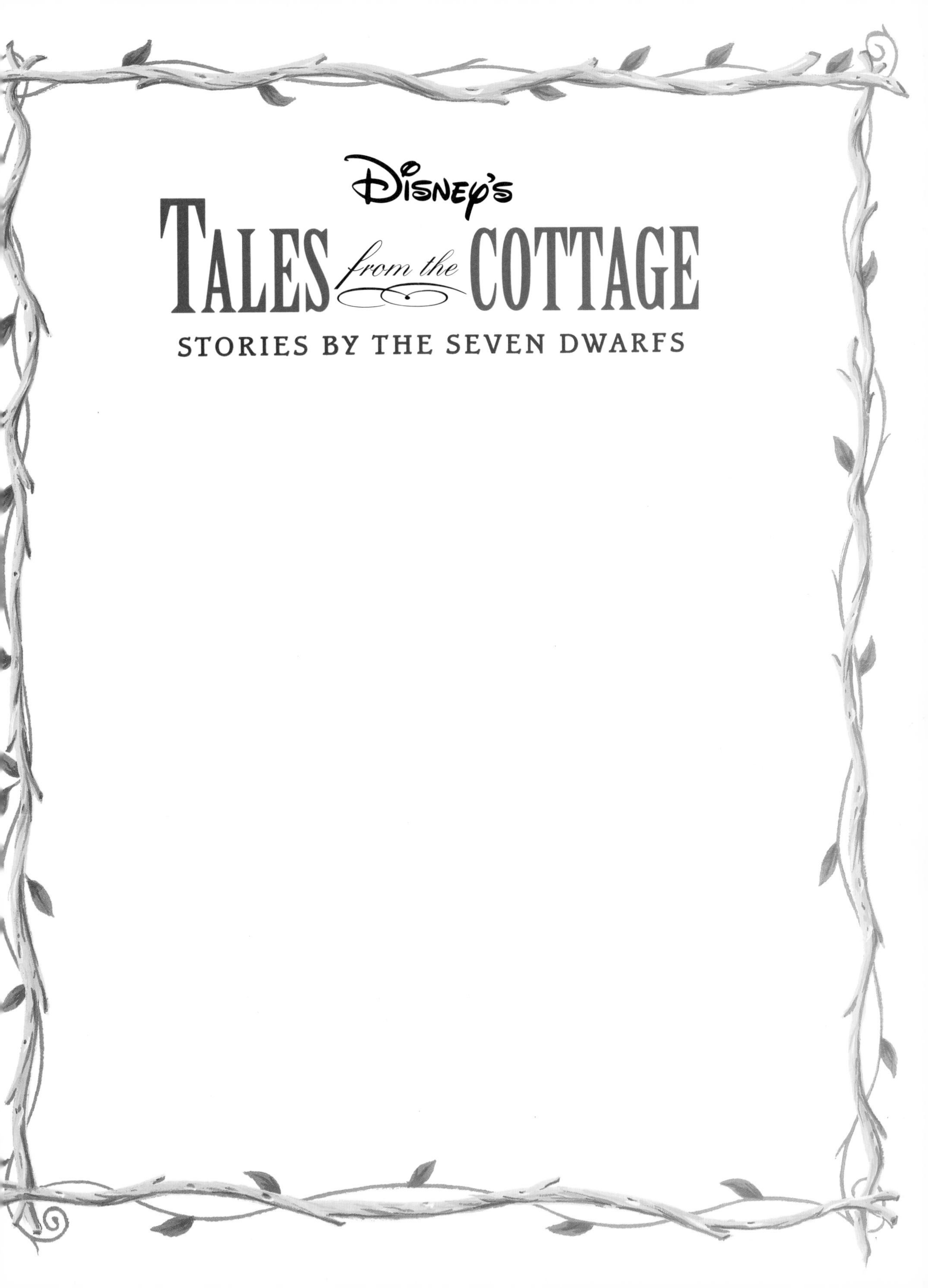

Disney's TALES from the COTTAGE

STORIES BY THE SEVEN DWARFS

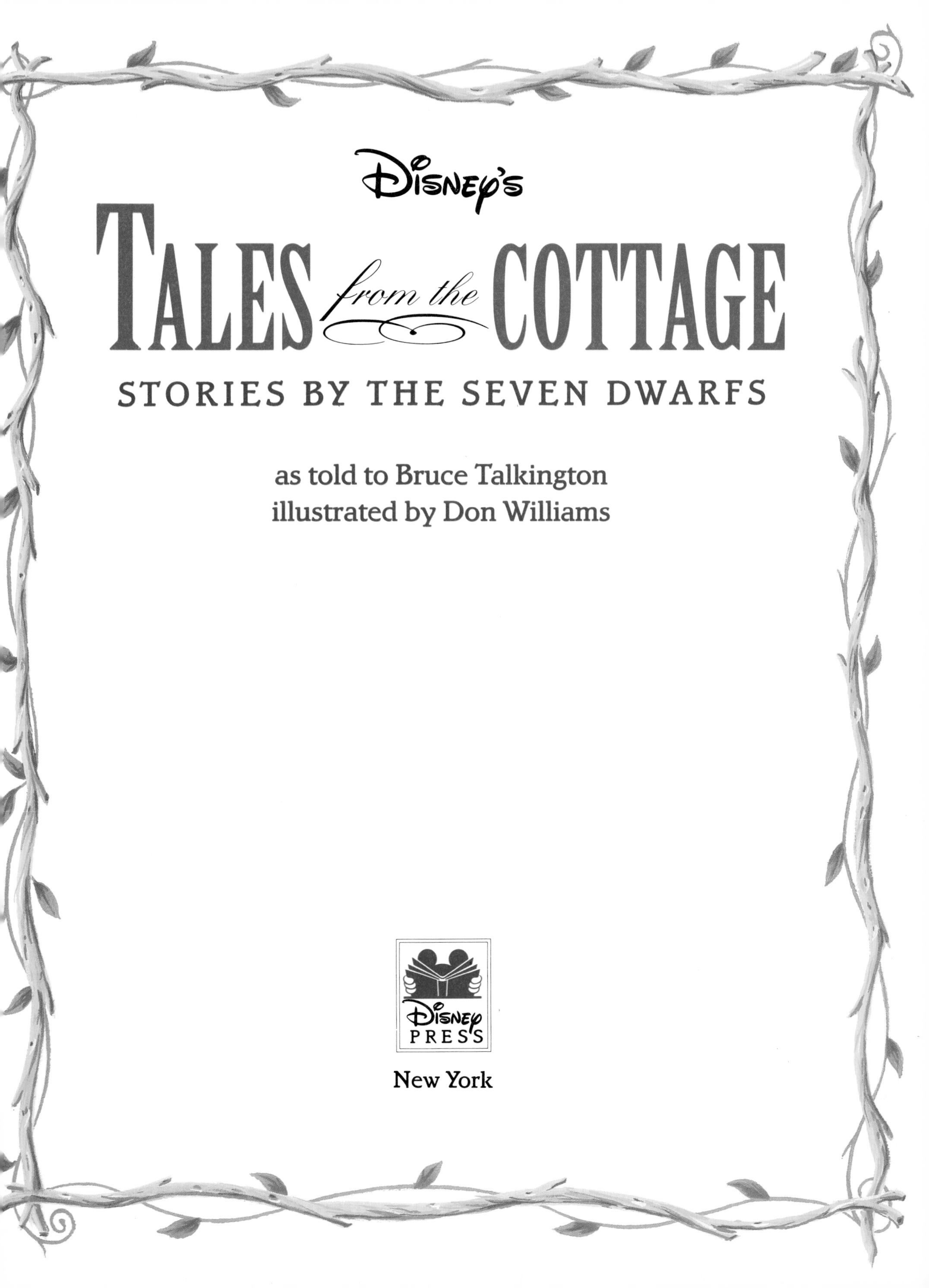

Disney's

TALES from the COTTAGE

STORIES BY THE SEVEN DWARFS

as told to Bruce Talkington
illustrated by Don Williams

Disney Press
New York

Printed in the United States of America.
For information address Disney Press, 114 Fifth Avenue,
New York, New York 10011.

First Edition

1 3 5 7 9 10 8 6 4 2

Library of Congress Catalog Card Number: 94-70813
ISBN 0-7868-3008-5/0-7868-5003-5 (lib. bdg.)

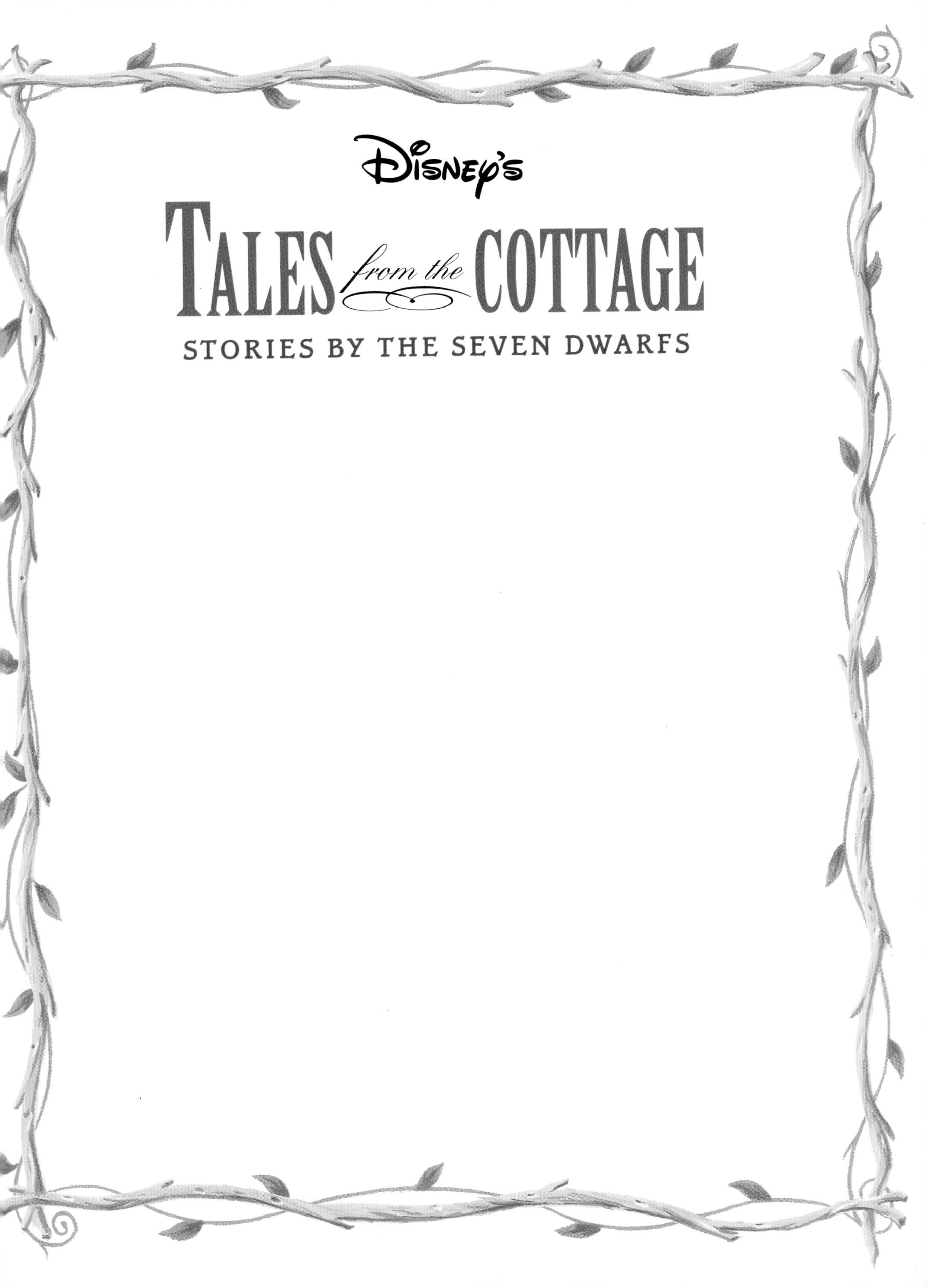

Disney's

TALES *from the* COTTAGE

STORIES BY THE SEVEN DWARFS

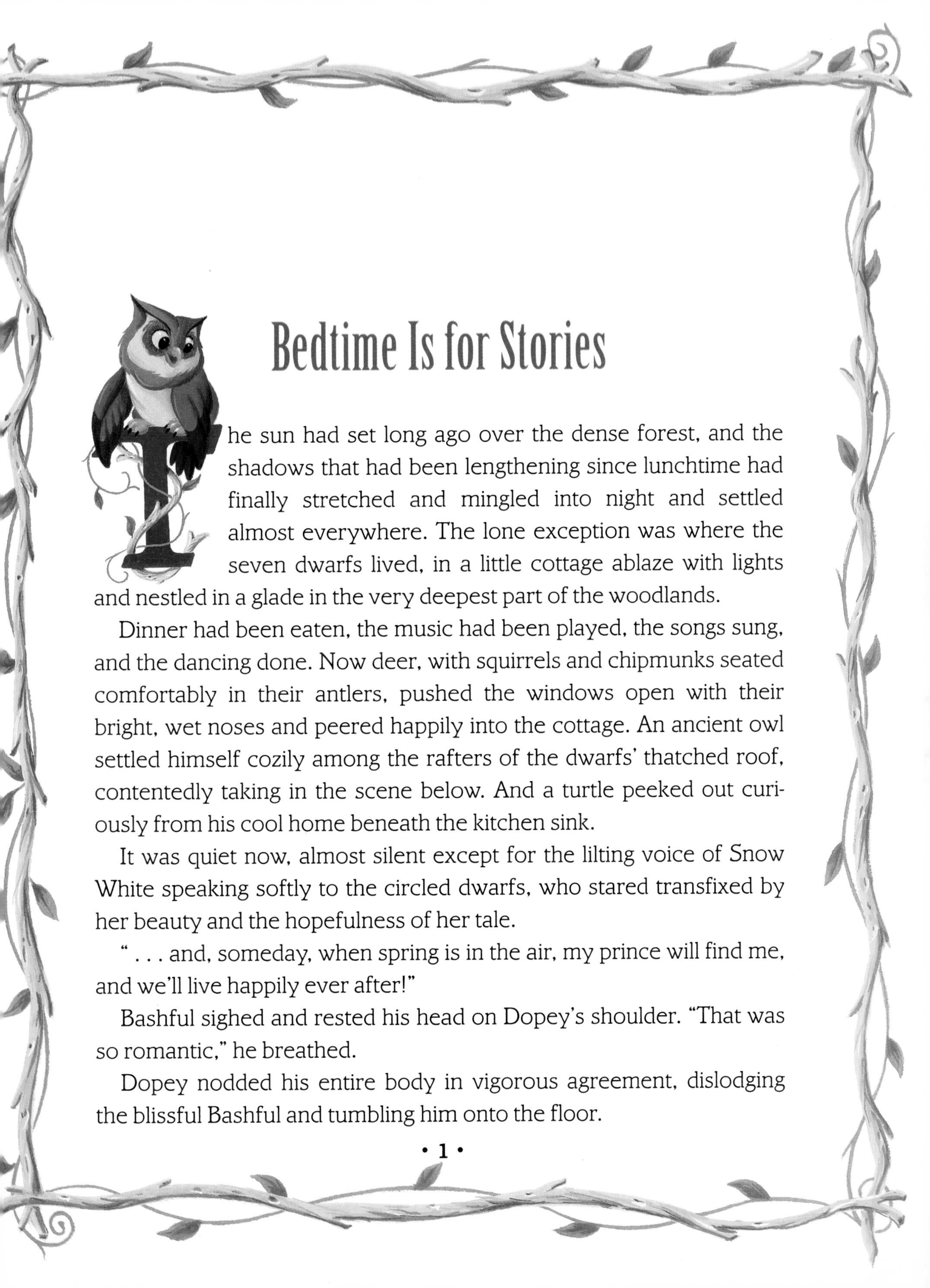

Bedtime Is for Stories

The sun had set long ago over the dense forest, and the shadows that had been lengthening since lunchtime had finally stretched and mingled into night and settled almost everywhere. The lone exception was where the seven dwarfs lived, in a little cottage ablaze with lights and nestled in a glade in the very deepest part of the woodlands.

Dinner had been eaten, the music had been played, the songs sung, and the dancing done. Now deer, with squirrels and chipmunks seated comfortably in their antlers, pushed the windows open with their bright, wet noses and peered happily into the cottage. An ancient owl settled himself cozily among the rafters of the dwarfs' thatched roof, contentedly taking in the scene below. And a turtle peeked out curiously from his cool home beneath the kitchen sink.

It was quiet now, almost silent except for the lilting voice of Snow White speaking softly to the circled dwarfs, who stared transfixed by her beauty and the hopefulness of her tale.

" . . . and, someday, when spring is in the air, my prince will find me, and we'll live happily ever after!"

Bashful sighed and rested his head on Dopey's shoulder. "That was so romantic," he breathed.

Dopey nodded his entire body in vigorous agreement, dislodging the blissful Bashful and tumbling him onto the floor.

Grumpy, not about to admit how much he liked the story, gave a disdainful sniff and grumbled, "Ah, mush!" much to Snow White's amusement. Her laughter filled the cottage until it was loudly interrupted by the chiming of the dwarfs' grandfather clock.

"Oh my goodness!" she exclaimed. "It's past your bedtime!"

"But we can't go to bed yet," yawned Sleepy.

"Certainly not," protested Doc.

Even Dopey shook his head.

"Why not?" asked Snow White with a smile.

Dopey scratched his head and shrugged.

The dwarfs exchanged desperate glances until Grumpy produced an explanation.

"It'd be rude," he growled. "*You* told *us* a story. We can't hit the sack until *you* hear *our* stories."

The dwarfs thumped Grumpy's back in such enthusiastic agreement that they knocked him off his chair.

"That's right," laughed Happy. "We know all sorts of stories about each other."

"But we're much too shy to tell our own . . . ," blushed Bashful.

" . . . so we'll tell you each other's!" finished Sneezy.

"Wonderful!" giggled Snow White, clapping her hands. "Which of you will be first?"

The dwarfs huddled together in a quick bout of whispering, and then the stories began.

Chapter One

Doc of All Trades

No one needs to ask why Grumpy is called Grumpy or why Dopey is known as Dopey. Happy is Happy because he is, Sneezy because he does, Bashful because he can't help himself, and Sleepy, of course, because he sleeps.

But why is Doc, the leader of the band of seven, called Doc? Unlike the others, it has nothing to do with what Mother Nature has done to him—made him grumpy, sneezy, sleepy, happy, dopey, or bashful. He's all those things at one time or another, just like most people. What makes Doc Doc is what *he* does for Mother Nature. He knows how to make things better. The creatures of the forest are keenly aware of this talent, and they do not hesitate to come to Doc with their problems, knowing that he will find a gentle solution in no time.

It was no surprise then when, early one morning, Doc tumbled boots over belt buckle down the front steps of the cottage in a desperate effort not to tromp on a brown lop-eared rabbit who was waiting patiently for him on the front porch.

"Let me guess," sighed Doc, looking up from the mud puddle in which he found himself sitting. "You've pot a goblin . . . er . . . I mean, got a problem. Am I right?"

In answer, the bunny immediately ceased scratching and headed for the forest, looking back to see if Doc was following. Doc climbed

to his feet, gave the seat of his soggy pants a squeeze, and loped after the rabbit. "I'm foming, cuzzy . . . uh, coming, fuzzy," Doc called to him, and they disappeared into the dark under the trees of the forest.

Doc had been following the rabbit for quite a long time when they came across a fox sitting in the middle of the forest path as if waiting for something. The exhausted bunny stopped and sat down, panting rapidly. "Pooped, eh, fuzzy?" Doc asked. "Well, can't say I blame you. I'm a little worn out myself, and my legs are lots longer than yours." He looked at the fox. "You the one with the problem, young fella?" As

if this were a signal, the fox jumped lightly to his feet and, with a flip of his bright red bushy tail, darted down a narrow trail leading deeper into the dark forest. The rabbit looked at Doc expectantly.

"I get it," said Doc, looking at the fox, then back at the waiting rabbit. "I'm supposed to follow ol' slyboots now, eh? Sort of a relay to gone me where I'm getting . . . er . . . get me where I'm going." And he winked knowingly. The rabbit winked back, and Doc set off down the trail with a laugh, trotting quickly to keep up with the fox, who was already just a flash of red among the green.

Doc was glad he had the fox's bright color to keep track of because they were traveling through a section of the forest where he had never been before. The now almost indistinguishable trail began leading upward into the foothills of the high mountains that loomed above the increasingly wild woodlands.

"Wait!" Doc called, finally having to stop and catch his breath. "Stop!" He pulled in a lungful of air. "Now I know how that rabbit felt."

At that moment the fox appeared in front of him, followed by a beautiful buck with the most magnificent set of antlers Doc had ever seen. "How am I supposed to follow him when I can't even keep up with you, red?" Doc asked the fox.

The buck reached out and caught Doc's sleeve with his teeth. He tugged and poked Doc with his nose, encouraging him to climb onto his back.

As soon as Doc had settled himself on the deer's broad back and gripped the antlers tightly, the buck broke into a powerful run, bounding effortlessly up the hillside with leaps that carried them both so high it seemed as if they were leaving the ground and taking flight.

The foothills were soon left behind, and Doc and the deer began climbing the mountains in earnest, leaving behind the trees and undergrowth until the increasing altitude left only rocky slopes strewn with boulders of immense size.

When Doc at last climbed gratefully off the buck's back at the foot of a steep wall of rock, he rubbed his backside vigorously. "Didn't know backbones could be so pointy," he remarked to the deer. But the buck had gone on his way, and Doc found himself staring into the eyes of the largest bear he'd ever seen.

"'Lo, bister mear . . . uh, mister bear," said Doc with a nervous smile. "Where to now?"

Without hesitation the bear clamped his teeth onto the back of

Doc's shirt and started climbing, carrying the dwarf like a mother cat totes a wayward kitten. Using his long, sharp claws, the bear made rapid time up the sheer face of the mountain. Doc tried to enjoy the ride. It was actually much less annoying than the deer's backbone if Doc kept his mind off what the bear might be considering for lunch.

The swinging to and fro from the bear's mouth became soothing after a while, and the weary dwarf soon fell asleep.

Doc was jolted awake when the bear dropped him on the floor of a huge cavern. Doc watched the bear wander off. He looked around. As far as he could tell, the dimly lit cave seemed to go on forever. There were the strangest formations of rock, besides the usual stalactites dangling like fangs from the ceiling and stalagmites pushing up to meet them from the floor. It appeared as if a sculptor had carved a dragon onto the nearest cave wall. But then the so-called carving turned and looked at Doc, letting out a hiss of warm, smoky breath as it took a sniff of the new visitor.

"Well," Doc gulped, "I soap you're the past . . . er . . . hope you're the last, 'cuz I don't think I want to meet what *you'd* be the messenger for."

The immense beast shifted her scaly body to one side, and Doc saw why he'd been summoned. A tiny dragon, about the size of an elephant, lay curled in the protective circle of his mother's body. When Doc saw the tear in his wing he breathed a sigh of relief. This was a situation he could handle.

Fumbling through his pockets (which were always kept filled with odds and ends for just such emergencies as this), Doc produced a large sewing needle and a spool of strong white thread. He knew that the dragon's wings were very much like fingernails and that the youngster would feel no pain, so he wasted no time in stitching up the long tear.

The baby dragon happily flexed his repaired wing, fanning a wave of air so powerful it almost blew Doc off his feet. The baby emitted a joyous screech to the large dragon, who responded with a tender roar that made the cave walls shiver.

Doc backed toward the entrance of the cave. "W-w-well," he stuttered nervously, "guess I'll be homing for head . . . uh, heading for home now that the job's done."

He turned and looked down the steep mountainside, realizing for the first time how far away from home he was.

"Shouldn't take more than two or three days . . . if I don't stop to eat or sleep," he sighed.

Then a giant claw closed gently around him, and the next thing Doc knew, the mother dragon had opened her wings and launched herself and her passenger high into the sky. Now that her offspring had been taken care of, she had no hesitation in carrying Doc home herself.

It seemed to Doc as if the entire world spread out before him as the dragon flew higher than it seemed possible for even clouds to reach. The trees looked like blades of grass, and lakes appeared little more than puddles. For a moment Doc thought he could reach out and touch the setting sun.

Back at the dwarfs' cottage, Doc's six companions were moping around a heavily laden dinner table, too worried about the missing dwarf to eat.

Suddenly there was a loud thump on the roof. Then the dwarfs heard Doc yell, and something began rolling off the soft thatch. As they rushed outside, there was a noisy splash from the yard.

They gathered around Doc, who was sitting, slightly dazed and very damp, in the large washtub.

"Why didn't you tell us you were taking a bath?" demanded Grumpy with relief. Then, noticing the surprised looks he was getting from the others, he scowled and added, "These tenderhearted doodlebugs were worried about you."

It seemed a little strange to them all that Doc had decided to wash with his clothes on, but they were much too polite to mention it. Besides, baths were something with which none of them were particularly familiar . . . and they wanted to keep it that way.

"It's dangerous taking a bath, especially this late at night," exclaimed Sleepy, as wide awake as anyone had ever seen him.

"Yeah," agreed Sneezy. "What if a bear had come along when your eyes were full of soap?"

"Or what if a dragon wandered up?" shivered Bashful.

Doc looked happily at the circle of anxious faces.

"Well, if that had happened," he responded thoughtfully, trying to keep a smile from spreading over his face, "I suppose I'd have needed a much larger washtub."

The other dwarfs ogled him in astonishment until Grumpy sniffed, "Oh, hogwash!"

Then the seven of them broke into a chorus of delighted laughter. Still chuckling, they trooped inside to share their belated dinner in front of the fire and listen to Doc relate his adventure as he dried the once-again soggy seat of his pants.

DOPEY

Chapter Two

The Nap Before Christmas

It was the night before Christmas, and not a creature was stirring in the cottage of the seven dwarfs . . . unless you count Sleepy. The droopy-eyed dwarf was tippy-toeing back and forth across the wooden floor in front of the fireplace, where seven stockings were dangling—more or less clean for a change—waiting for the arrival of everyone-knows-who.

Of all the dwarfs, Sleepy was the last one anyone would expect to wait up and meet Santa Claus—especially after what inevitably proved to be the most exhausting day of the year. Wrapping presents, helping prepare the Christmas dinner for the next afternoon, cleaning out the fireplace, and sweeping a year's worth of soot out of the chimney to make Santa's visit more pleasant were all quite strenuous activities. And when one added the magical excitement of the holiday itself, well, all the dwarfs were stretching and yawning well before bedtime and quite willing to call it an early night. In no time at all they were all tucked snugly into their little beds, a contented chorus of snores filling the air as they dreamed happy dreams of the next morning.

Everyone was dreaming except Sleepy, that is. This was what he'd been waiting for all year long. He was determined to be wide awake when Santa arrived, to shake his hand, and to thank him in person for all his present-laden visits over the years. And although a personal

thank-you to Santa was a nice idea, it wasn't the main reason Sleepy had decided to wait up.

It all came down to the simple fact that Sleepy was—and always would be—Sleepy. He'd spent his entire life sleeping through exciting moments, interesting events, and happenings of great importance. And the only reason he'd never really missed anything was that his six friends—yes, even Grumpy—had always taken great care and kindness to describe in generous and loving detail what had taken place while Sleepy had been snoozing.

Sleepy felt the very best Christmas present he could offer in return was the story of Santa coming to call. If only he could keep himself awake—all that was being accomplished by his pacing back and forth was that he was becoming more and more weary.

"I'll never stay awake if I keep this up," he sighed, struggling to stifle a yawn. "Santa'll be here and gone again between snores!"

It was when he opened the windows and settled himself on the most uncomfortable chair he could find (hoping the cold winter drafts would keep him alert) that Sleepy discovered he wasn't the only one stirring on Christmas Eve after all. The woodland creatures were as interested as the dwarfs themselves in what Santa was bringing, and they didn't seem to be having any trouble staying awake. This immediately perked Sleepy up and gave him an idea that he put to work at once.

With the assistance of the forest animals, Sleepy tried everything to keep awake. First he convinced the squirrels to play leapfrog while he attempted to count them *backward*, hoping this would make him less inclined to doze. It didn't work. Snowballs on his lap proved *quite* effective for a while but soon melted away and left him not only as drowsy as before but much soggier. It didn't appear as if Sleepy would make it until morning.

As soon as Sleepy's eyes closed, however, and he began to snore gently, the chipmunks who lived in a nearby hollow oak scampered into action. Climbing through an open window, they scurried up onto the table next to Sleepy and with great care poured a glass of cold water down the collar of his shirt.

Sleepy was not sleepy for quite some time after that. But it was a long night, and eventually Sleepy was once again sprawled loosely on his chair, feet propped up on the table, his gentle snores filling the night.

This time two deer, an antlered buck and his smaller, more delicate mate, pushed open the front door with their noses and crossed the room to Sleepy, their hooves clicking lightly on the wooden floor.

Sleepy didn't miss a snore or move a muscle as the deer each took the toe of one of the dwarf's soft leather boots between their teeth and gently tugged them off. A couple of the leapfrogging squirrels then backed up to Sleepy's bare feet and began brushing the bottoms with their soft, bushy tails. In no time at all Sleepy's snores turned to giggles, then to chuckles, and finally to outright laughter. The sound of his own happy laughter awakened him.

Morning was still hours away, but as far as Sleepy could tell, Santa had not yet arrived. Sleepy dozed off again with his chin resting on his hands in the mistaken belief that sitting up would be enough to keep him awake. The ancient owl who lived among the rafters of the dwarfs' cottage flew down and perched on the table directly in front of Sleepy's face. When he asked, "Who?" in his owllike way, all he got for his pains was a loud snore.

Taking one of the long feathers from his soft, shiny wings, the owl gently began to tickle Sleepy's nose with it. The dwarf's nose twitched one way, then another, and yet another in a vain attempt to avoid the irritating feather. It was no use, however, and sooner than even the owl expected, Sleepy cut loose with a sneeze that blew the owl across the room and out the kitchen window.

It was such a loud sneeze that the soundly sleeping dwarfs upstairs said, "Bless you!" to the surprised Sneezy, who thanked them, then went back to sleep wondering why he couldn't recall having just sneezed a sneeze that had woken up all his friends.

That sneeze kept Sleepy awake and alert for quite some time. Finally, though, the wait became too much for everyone. Sleepy was stretched out on his chair with the chipmunks asleep in his shirt pockets, the squirrels curled up on his lap, and the deer dozing on their feet next to the warm stove in the cozy kitchen.

No one stirred as a figure dressed in a sooty red suit trimmed with white fur dropped down the chimney, easily avoiding the dying embers in the fireplace, and set his huge pack on the hearth. He looked at the sleeping dwarf and the animals and knew without being told what Sleepy was up to. He walked right over to the napping dwarf and shook him lightly by the shoulder.

Sleepy opened one droopy eyelid and saw the smiling, bearded face with bright eyes twinkling down into his own. Instantly both of

Sleepy's eyes popped open in amazement and delight. Santa had arrived. And Sleepy was awake to see him!

Before he could say anything, however, Santa put his finger to his lips, and—after helping Sleepy lay aside the sleeping animals—he pulled him over to his pack. Without a word passing between them, Santa began producing gifts from the depths of his bag and handing them to Sleepy, indicating into which dwarf's stocking each was to be placed.

There was a pouch with his name on it for Doc to keep handy whatever he might need on his errands of mercy.

Happy was getting a new leather belt with a bright, silvery buckle that wouldn't burst at his next belly laugh.

Bashful was to receive a beautiful black satin blindfold so he could trim his beard without being embarrassed by his own image in the mirror.

Sneezy got handkerchiefs, of course: seven different colors so he'd have a clean one for every day of the week.

Santa had brought Dopey a yo-yo because he knew how much fun all the dwarfs would have taking turns teaching him how to use it.

And Grumpy received an enormous hand mirror to practice the fierce scowls that no one took seriously in the least.

Then, with a wink, Santa pulled Sleepy's present out of the pack. It was the largest, softest, most delicately embroidered pillow Sleepy had ever seen. He opened his mouth to thank Santa but again was motioned to silence. Santa was always delighted to be waited up for, but he also knew night was for sleeping—even the night before Christmas.

Taking Sleepy by the arm, he settled him comfortably on his new pillow and was back up the chimney with his pack before Sleepy was aware he was leaving. Sleepy was aware of hardly anything at all—

except the sweet-smelling softness of his present. He was sound asleep before Santa had even crossed the dwarfs' thatched roof to his waiting sleigh.

And that was the way Sleepy's six companions found him the next morning, sleeping peacefully, surrounded by his woodland friends. He

didn't even awaken when the other dwarfs opened their stockings and whooped their delight at what they found.

But later, at breakfast, when Sleepy was awake, they all had a wonderful time as he gave them his present—the story, in glorious detail, of the adventure they had all slept through.

Chapter Three

Snow Time for Fun

"Don't be dilly, Soapy . . . er . . . silly, Dopey," Doc gently admonished his friend. Doc stood before the huge fire roaring in the cottage's hearth, warming his hands and feet. "It's snowing outside."

"Been snowing for days," added Sneezy, dabbing at his glowing red nose with a brightly colored handkerchief. "We couldn't get the door open even if we wanted to go outside . . . which we *don't*." He gave a little shiver at the thought of it.

Dopey walked over to where Grumpy was passing the time whittling a piece of wood into toothpicks and tugged hopefully on Grumpy's sleeve.

"They're right for a change," answered Grumpy, looking up from his carving. "There's nothing to do when it's snowing but to wait for it to stop."

Dopey frowned with disappointment, then shook his head.

"Suit yourself, Dopey," answered Grumpy with a shrug. He wagged his stick at Dopey. "But if you're bored and looking for something to do, the middle of a snowstorm is the last place you'll find it. Humpf!"

Dopey, however, was convinced that anything—even a snowstorm—had to be better than being cooped up in a cottage with half a dozen bored dwarfs. He pulled on his heaviest pair of boots and donned several thick sweaters. Then he wrapped a long knitted muffler around

his neck and stretched a rainbow-hued stocking cap over his head and ears. Grinning happily, Dopey felt he was fully prepared for his winter adventure—whatever it turned out to be.

Dopey clomped up the stairs, pushed open a second-story window, and viewed the huge drifts of snow piled against the cottage. Sneezy had been right. The doors and all the windows on the lower floor were completely blocked by snow. The only way to the outside was through an upstairs window.

Without a second thought, Dopey climbed over the windowsill and hopped down onto what he thought was a solid drift of snow.

Sploosh! Dopey sank into the snow and disappeared as silently as a pebble tossed into a pond. A moment later, however, he rolled out from the bottom of the heap of snow looking very much like a tiny snowman. Then, sputtering and gasping, he began shaking off the snow like a dog shrugging off water after a bath. Dopey blinked excitedly. He was outside. All he needed now was to find something to do besides shiver.

Taking a large step, Dopey was startled when he lost his footing on the slippery snow and came down with a bump on his heavily padded bottom.

Dopey got up and shuffled his feet frantically. He was bewildered to discover that although he was running furiously on the icy snow he wasn't going anywhere. Both feet suddenly skidded out from under him, and there he was once more, sitting in the snow.

Dopey climbed to his feet again and stood as stiff as a statue, afraid to move for fear of falling. But as he stood, barely daring to breathe, Dopey suddenly realized he was slowly slithering down the slippery incline that sloped toward the shed, where the dwarfs stored their tools.

Dopey turned and tried to walk back up the hill, but his feet began

slipping and sliding again, and the faster he moved his feet, the faster he slid toward the shed. Suddenly he lost his footing altogether and began racing down the hill like a runaway toboggan.

All at once there was a *crash!* as Dopey burst through the door and

cartwheeled across the floor. He glanced dizzily around the inside of the shed. It was a shambles. Rakes, hoes, spades, brushes, and dozens of barrel staves were scattered everywhere. Buckets of paint and pots of glue had been upended and were dripping onto the floor.

Horrified, Dopey jumped to his feet and began scrambling about, furiously straightening up the mess he had made. If there was anything the dwarfs disliked more than dinner being late, it was an untidy toolshed. Dirty dishes, grimy clothes, cobwebs, or unswept floors didn't bother them. But finding a tool out of place? That was different! Tools were something all the dwarfs took very seriously.

"Take care of your tools, Dopey," Doc was forever telling him, "and they'll take care of you!"

Dopey quickly returned the rakes and hoes and picks and shovels to their ordered rows against the walls. He set all the buckets, pots, and brushes neatly back on their appropriate shelves. But then Dopey

noticed that large globs of glue were smeared all over his boots. Tracking mud through the cottage was an everyday affair that none of the dwarfs thought twice about. But the toolshed floor had to be kept spotless.

Thinking quickly, Dopey brought each boot down onto a barrel stave. Dopey smiled, realizing that this way no glue would be tracked across the floor.

Then something curious happened when Dopey took a step toward the open door. That is, when he *tried* to take a step. His feet were stuck fast to the flat slats of wood! He kicked, twisted, and pulled, but the boots would not come unstuck.

Frowning with determination, Dopey reached down and firmly grasped the tips of the barrel staves. Then, taking a deep breath, he kicked with all his might.

Instead of his boots pulling free from the wood, Dopey found himself somersaulting spectacularly through the door of the shed. When the slats of wood hit the slick snow, Dopey was terrified to suddenly find himself skiing rapidly through the trees that surrounded the cottage. Each time Dopey tried to slow himself down by reaching out wildly to grasp a small tree or sapling, he would be sent spinning in circles. When he released the tree he would shoot off in an entirely different direction.

Soon, however, Dopey discovered how simple it was to maneuver on his skis, and he stopped being afraid and began to enjoy himself thoroughly.

Soon Dopey was gliding back and forth across the clearing quite fearlessly. He even skied up the drift surrounding the cottage, rattled over the roof, and zipped down the other side.

Hearing the commotion, the other dwarfs looked on in wonder as Dopey spun and swirled across the snow.

The next thing Dopey knew, his friends had tumbled out the upstairs window and gathered around him, full of questions.

"Where'd you get those doohickeys?" asked Sleepy, wide awake.

"Are there more?" Sneezy sniffed.

"How'd you learn to use 'em?" Happy asked.

"When do I get a turn?" Grumpy wanted to know.

For the remainder of that winter and for all the winters that came after, the dwarfs were no longer trapped in their cottage by snow or weighed down by boredom.

And when it came to winter's first snowfall and the question of who was to be the first to cross the trackless white surface and celebrate its arrival, the choice was always unanimous . . . Dopey!

Chapter Four
Sneezy's Story

A*-chooo!"*

There was never any difficulty identifying the arrival of spring at the cottage of the seven dwarfs. The first humongous sneeze of the season would blast the dwarfs out of their beds and tumble them onto the floor in a dazed pile. From there they would look up at the embarrassed Sneezy as he vigorougly applied a handkerchief to his nose.

"Sorry, fellas," he would sniff. "Must be that time of year again."

So spring would make its noisy arrival as Sneezy's ordinarily modest snuffles and sneezles were suddenly transformed into powerful gusts of wind. And from that moment to the end of summer, Sneezy's six friends had to be constantly on their toes because they never knew when an oversize sneeze was going to happen.

But the most annoying things often bring along some good things as well. Spring and Sneezy were no exception.

"I suppose," one dwarf or another would casually ask Sneezy, "that you're going to do it again this year?"

"Of course," Sneezy would answer, getting that faraway look in his eyes that meant the one thing all the dwarfs could hardly wait through the winter for—*flowers!*

At the very back of the dwarfs' vegetable garden, behind the turnips, right alongside the butter beans, a patch of ground was set

aside just for Sneezy. Every spring in this plot of moist black earth Sneezy would plant, water, weed, and wait patiently for his flowers to bloom and fill the dwarfs' lives with color and perfume . . . and more sneezes.

"A-chooo!"

"There goes another shutter," Sleepy would sigh.

"Well," Doc would respond as he picked up his toolbox, "better it happened now than in the middle of a gizzard . . . er . . . blizzard this winter."

"A-chooo!"

"Omigosh!" Bashful would exclaim. "That one twisted Grumpy up in the hammock tighter than a cocoon on a caterpillar!"

"A-chooo!"

"He just blew all the apples off our tree," Happy pointed out in wonder.

"We'd've had to pick 'em sooner or later, anyway," grumbled Grumpy. "Now will somebody get me out of this hammock?"

"But we *wouldn't* have dropped them all on Dopey when we did it," Doc would remark as he put down his toolbox and went to fetch a soothing something to rub onto the bumps raised on poor Dopey's head by the falling apples.

The more spectacular the flowers blooming under Sneezy's tender attentions, the more spectacular the sneezes that battered the dwarfs.

Then, on a day when the flowers in Sneezy's garden had never

been more numerous or arrayed in brighter colors—a day when Sneezy had never been happier—things were turned upside down in that tiny trace of time it took to sneeze. It was a hurricane in a hurry, a gale in a heartbeat, a tempest in quick time. One moment Sneezy was gathering a huge bouquet to adorn the dinner table, and the next moment . . .

"A-choooooo!"

. . . the air was full of floating flower petals, and the thatched roof of the cottage had disappeared as if it had never been.

Even an entire thatched roof is not much to repair when more than half a dozen determined dwarfs pitch in together. Besides, what was a little roof, an occasional shutter, a minor cave-in at work in comparison to Sneezy and his flowers? The dwarfs made short work of the project with no grumbling from any of them . . . well, almost.

Sneezy, looking around at his friends, who were bedraggled and weary from having to devote their spare time to repairing yet another mess resulting directly from one of his sneezes, decided enough was enough.

"Why should my very best friends have to suffer from my sneezing?" Sneezy said to himself. "That's pretty selfish . . . isn't it?"

"I'm never going to sneeze again," he announced to the amazement of his companions.

"But you're Sneezy," protested Doc. "That's what you do. Just like Happy is happy, Sleepy's sleepy. . . . "

"We can't be mad at anyone just for being himself," agreed Happy. "Not even Grumpy."

"I should hope not," Grumpy sniffed disdainfully. He then added, "Listen to 'em, Sneezy. They're makin' sense"—he lifted a bushy eyebrow—"for a change."

But Sneezy was determined. He shook his head vigorously and readjusted the extremely large clothespin he had fastened to his nose. He wasn't taking any chances.

"Nobody else has to be cleaned up after," he argued.

"But," inquired Bashful in a tiny voice, "what about our flowers?" The shy dwarf had brought up a good point. If Sneezy were going to avoid sneezing, he would have to give up his garden. And that was something they all would miss, because it was almost as much a part of Sneezy as were his very sneezes themselves. In comparison to his specialness, what were a few high winds? But Sneezy was certain he was right and wouldn't listen.

In no time at all the cottage was peaceful but full of miserable dwarfs. Sneezy's friends realized that if they didn't get him sneezing again, they would all be sitting around feeling sorry for themselves forever.

"Something's got to be done," Grumpy thundered, pounding his fist on the table, "and it's got to be done now . . . if not sooner!" No one missed the flowers and the smile on Sneezy's face more than he did.

But what were they going to do?

"If we can get him sneezing again," suggested Happy, "he'll remember how much he misses it."

"And how much we *all* miss his flowers," added Bashful.

"How do we get him to sneeze when he doesn't want to?" sighed Doc.

Dopey came up with an idea. He thought the handful-of-pepper-under-the-nose trick was the answer. Unfortunately, Dopey wanted to be absolutely certain it would work and took a trial sniff.

"A-chooo!"

Dopey's sneeze filled the air with pepper, and all six dwarfs launched into sneezing fits.

Happy had heard somewhere that tickling the inside of someone's ear with a feather would coax out a sneeze. The others thought it a strange approach at best, but because it didn't involve any handfuls of pepper, they were in favor of giving it a try and waited until Sneezy was taking an afternoon nap. All Happy got for his efforts was losing the feather in the depths of Sneezy's ear.

Doc tried the services of a fuzzy black-and-yellow-striped bumblebee buzzing under Sneezy's nose with pollen-laden wings. Before the bee could get started, however, he was sniffed into Sneezy's nose in a stupendous snore when Doc removed the clothespin.

Fortunately, the bee was quite unharmed and managed to find his

way out through Sneezy's ear, bringing Happy back his feather in the process.

Sleepy had a wonderful idea for sneeze making but fell asleep and couldn't remember what it was. Luckily he'd confided it to Bashful before dropping off, but Bashful was too embarrassed to follow through with the plan himself, so he whispered it to Grumpy.

Grumpy thought it was a splendid idea and wasted no time putting it into effect. He led the others into the abandoned flower garden, where each of the six dwarfs collected a huge bouquet of flowers—pansies in velvet waistcoats, laughing daffodils, blue-eyed violets, and Sneezy's favorites, crisp yellow snapdragons.

These bouquets were spread over the sleeping dwarf in the certainty that the rainbow blooms would coax a sneeze from him. The dwarfs waited and waited, but Sneezy merely kept snoring away without a sniffle or a sputter.

The dwarfs didn't have any idea what to do next when Sneezy suddenly opened his eyes and gave a mighty yawn. Then he noticed the flowers, and a smile spread over his face like dawn suddenly shining through a picture window. He gently gathered the flowers to him and rubbed his face happily against the soft petals.

Sneezy began to giggle, then to chuckle, and finally to laugh outright. And in the midst of his laughter came . . . a sneeze. Then another. And another until it was impossible to distinguish where the laughter ended and the sneezes began.

It was at this time that the dwarfs made the great discovery: Sneezy didn't sneeze because there was something *wrong* with his *nose;* Sneezy sneezed because everything was *right* with his *heart.*

"And it would be pretty selfish not to share what makes us happy with each other, now wouldn't it?" Happy pointed out as he patted Sneezy on the back.

Sneezy, who hadn't looked at it that way at all, nodded with relief. "I suppose," Sneezy responded thoughtfully, "that stifling sneezes is as silly as stifling happiness."

"It is to us," murmured Grumpy. "There's nothing worse than havin' a sourpuss hangin' around all the time."

"You ought to know, Grumpy," laughed Happy, and all the dwarfs joined in the merriment.

"Never mind them, Sneezy," said Grumpy with a twinkle in his eye as he put his arm around Sneezy's shoulders. "Let's go pick some posies for the dinner table."

"A-chooo!" Sneezy agreed happily.

Chapter Five

Silence Is Golden

"Are you *absolutely* sure it's my turn?" Bashful asked.

Doc tickled the inside of his ear with the fluffy feather of his quill pen and squinted carefully at the paper in his hand.

"There's no doubt about it, Bashful," Doc replied. "Everyone's teen to bown, I mean, been to town but you. Happy's been *twice.* It's definitely your turn."

"I'd be more than glad to wait," offered Bashful, glancing hopefully at the other dwarfs, "if anyone wanted to go in my place?"

"You have to go sometime, Bashful," said Grumpy. "You may as well get it over with."

Sneezy put his arm around Bashful's shoulders. "None of us really enjoys going to town, Bashful," he said, sniffing, "but we have to sell the jewels from our mine."

"But you're all so much better at selling than I am," Bashful protested timidly. "Even Dopey."

"How do you know that?" asked Sleepy, stifling a yawn. "You've never been to town to try."

"Oh, I know," said Bashful, sighing. "But I even have a hard time talking to you fellas . . . and *you're* my best friends." He gave a little shiver. "How am I supposed to talk to complete strangers, let alone convince them to buy something?" He shook his head in despair.

"We all agreed to take our turn, good or bad," Grumpy reminded him, waving his finger around importantly.

"You're right, Grumpy," moaned Bashful, "but that sure doesn't make it any easier."

"Just do the best you can," Grumpy responded. The other dwarfs nodded in agreement. "We can't ask for more than that, can we?"

Grumpy said, and punched Bashful lightly on the shoulder, which, coming from Grumpy, was sympathy indeed.

"Well," Bashful mumbled, "if my best is all you're expecting, then you can't be expecting much." He filled the air with a long, drawn-out sigh. "Thank goodness for that."

Bashful arrived at the market town a few days later carrying a sack

of gemstones on his back. The marketplace was even worse than Bashful had imagined. The jostling crowds of strangers, the closely packed buildings, the bustling lanes and thoroughfares packed end to end with carts and wagons and other horsedrawn contraptions frightened Bashful like nothing he'd ever seen before.

"Oh noooo," groaned Bashful. "I'll *never* be able to sell anything here. I may as well just go home right now."

Bashful gave a hopeless sigh. In fact, he'd actually turned around and was looking longingly down the road that led back to the forest when, all at once, a large hand fell heavily on his shoulder.

"You must be Bashful," came a deep, laughing voice. "We've been expecting you!"

Bashful looked up in bewilderment and found himself suddenly in the center of a boisterous group of very tall men. At least, they *seemed* awfully tall to Bashful. But then, pretty much everyone seemed tall to him.

"We're very happy to see you, Bashful," said the man as he took Bashful's hand and shook it warmly. He had a huge, bushy mustache and a wide, smiling mouth, and his head was as bald as a hard-boiled egg.

"Yes," agreed another man. He was so very round that when he laughed, Bashful was afraid the button holding up his pants might pop off. "You're the only one of the seven we haven't met," he said. "We thought you were never coming to town."

"Your six friends have made quite an impression around here," chuckled a third man. He was so thin that when he turned sideways all Bashful noticed was his immense feet in their shiny black leather shoes and bright silver buckles.

"Come along with us, Bashful," said the first man. "We'll be delighted to get you settled in."

"And we'll help you set up your stall so you can start selling your jewels," added the very thin man.

"Thank you very much," whispered Bashful, casting a last, yearning glance at the road and the trees in the distance.

"Don't mention it," chuckled the round man, giving Bashful a friendly slap on the back. "It's always a special occasion when one of the seven dwarfs comes to visit."

In no time at all Bashful's new friends had him firmly established under a brightly striped canvas awning, seated behind a table covered with sparkling jewels. He was surrounded by dozens of other salesmen in similar stalls shouting at the hundreds and hundreds of customers thronging up and down the narrow lanes of the market.

"We'll leave you on your own now," said the man with the bushy mustache.

"Yes, you don't need our help anymore," agreed his friend with the silver buckles.

"No dwarf ever needed anyone's help selling his wares," chuckled the man with the button on his pants. "Good-bye, Bashful. It was nice meeting you."

Bashful gave a weak smile of thanks and an embarrassed wave as his new friends left him and disappeared into the crowd. He looked around at the yelling salesmen and hung his head in despair. "How am I going to sell anything?" he asked himself meekly. "I can't coax and bully complete strangers into even *looking* at my gems, let alone talk them into buying them." He let out a great sigh and shook his head forlornly. "It's hopeless," he groaned miserably.

"Say," came an unfamiliar voice, "aren't you the quiet one?"

Bashful looked up. A small, trim man in a neat tweed jacket and

matching knickers was looking at him owlishly through a huge pair of spectacles.

"Goods not worth shouting about, eh?"

Bashful tried to speak, but nothing came out. Instead, he shrugged—and blushed.

The man considered the sparkling stones spread out on the table. "Or are they *so* good that they can speak for themselves?" the man wondered, suddenly looking shrewdly at Bashful.

Bashful swallowed hard. "Well . . . ," he squeaked.

Quickly the man examined first one stone, then another. "Why, these jewels are remarkable!" he gasped. "Superb!" he roared. "Stupendous. Magnificent! No wonder you're so confident and don't have to shout."

The man's enthusiasm instantly attracted the attention of the crowd, and before Bashful knew it, he was overwhelmed with customers at his stall clamoring to buy his jewels at any price.

By lunchtime Bashful had sold every jewel in his sack—*and* he had received much more than any of the dwarfs would have expected. He arrived back home at the cottage just as his friends were sitting down to dinner. They shook their heads sadly and exchanged knowing glances to see Bashful back so soon. They gathered around him with words of comfort.

"Never mind," said Doc. "It's always difficult the first time."

"You'll do better next time," Happy assured him, and Dopey nodded and patted Bashful gently on the back.

"Didn't you manage to sell anything?" barked Grumpy.

A smile suddenly split Bashful's face from ear to ear. "Some," Bashful said shyly. He turned his sack upside down and dumped the coins onto the table.

"Ahhhh!" said the other dwarfs simultaneously.

When their amazement wore off, they let out a cheer that nearly lifted the roof off the cottage. They hoisted Bashful onto their shoulders and marched him around the room in triumph. Finally, after the cheering died down, Grumpy came forward and looked Bashful directly in the eye.

"I wasn't going to ask you how you did it," he sniffed, "but the other fellas really want to know. So . . . how'd you do it?"

Bashful looked down and gave his familiar, embarrassed shrug. "I guess . . . ," he began.

All the other dwarfs leaned forward, straining to hear. "What d'you guess?" asked Grumpy impatiently.

Bashful smiled. "I guess I'm just a born salesman."

And with that, Bashful blushed from head to toe—and wouldn't say another word.

Chapter Six

Grumpy's Story

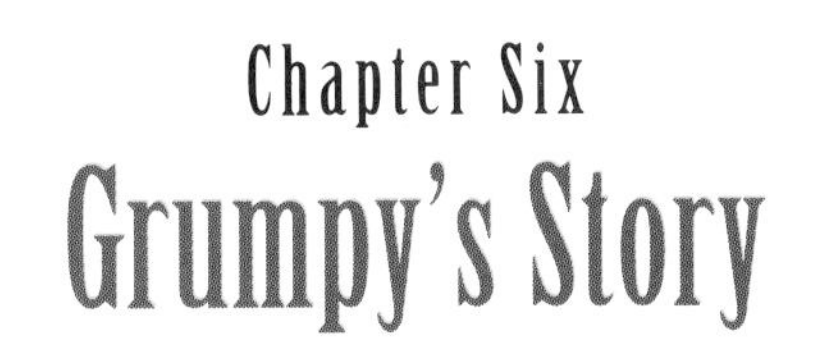

Why are you so grumpy all the time?" Bashful asked Grumpy quite out of the blue one afternoon. If anyone but Bashful had asked him this question, Grumpy wouldn't have bothered to answer. But Bashful's feelings were easily hurt, and feelings were not something people went around hurting on purpose, not even if one's name was Grumpy.

"I'm not grumpy all the time!" he protested.

"But we call you Grumpy all the time," reasoned Bashful.

"Well, I am *Grumpy* all the time," explained Grumpy, his brow wrinkling thoughtfully, "but I'm not *grumpy* all the time, see?"

"Ah," said Bashful, nodding his head, pretending he understood. "But how do you *know* you're not grumpy all the time?"

Grumpy couldn't answer that. *Was* he grumpy all the time? he wondered He didn't think so. Oh sure, he admitted to himself, he *looked* grumpy all the time, but all pulled down in a frown was just the way his face worked. That didn't mean he was *feeling* all pulled down in a frown. Or did it? Now Grumpy was thoroughly confused. All he knew was that he didn't *want* to be grumpy all the time.

It was a bothersome puzzle, and Grumpy decided to take a stroll in the woods to see if he could figure it out. He chose a path that ran alongside a mountain stream. Rushing down from the upper reaches

of the forest, the stream was swollen with melted snow, and the water crashed and swirled and tumbled over the many rocks and boulders that filled the stream.

Grumpy enjoyed the music of the cheerfully rushing water. It was doing exactly what it was supposed to do, Grumpy told himself, and letting the entire forest know about it. That's why he enjoyed roaming alone in the woods. Everything was in its place; trees treed, streams

streamed, and water whooshed without having to explain themselves to anyone. To Grumpy it was all very soothing and comfortable. No one had to be grumpy out in the wild—not even him.

But was he being grumpy anyway?

Moving beside the splashing stream, Grumpy studied his reflection in a quiet pool among the boulders.

"Humpf," he snorted. "Looks pretty grumpy to me, all right."

Before he could consider this any further, however, Grumpy heard a strange noise above the roar of the rushing water.

"Peep! Peep!"

Not far away, Grumpy discovered a tiny bird at the foot of a tree on the bank of the stream.

"Peep! Peep!" chirped the bird, staring up at Grumpy out of shiny black eyes.

"Peep peep yourself!" responded Grumpy. As tenderly as he could, Grumpy lifted the bird from the damp grass and cupped him cozily in his calloused hands.

"What's the matter, buster?" Grumpy whispered. The tiny bird was still too young for feathers but was covered in a fine coat of soft fluff. "You lost?"

Leaning back and shading his eyes, Grumpy could just make out a nest neatly constructed of woven twigs and leaves far above the forest floor in the branches of the tree.

"Too small to fly, but too big to sit still and keep from falling, eh?" Grumpy remarked.

"Peep! Peep!" replied the bird, as if in agreement.

"Well, down here is no place for the likes of you, that's for sure and certain," Grumpy said, and sighed. "And since you can't fly, I suppose ol' Grumpy's going to have to climb, eh?"

"Peep! Peep!"

Grumpy carefully wrapped the bird in his handkerchief and tucked him comfortably into the pocket of his shirt. Then, after spitting on his hands, he began to climb the tree toward the nest high above him.

Halfway up the tree, however, Grumpy stepped on a rotten branch. *Crack!* went the branch, and down went Grumpy into the rushing river. *Splash!*

Grumpy spluttered and sputtered as he felt himself being swept down the river. Kicking his legs to keep afloat, Grumpy plucked the

tiny bird out of his pocket and held him above the water that was carrying them downstream.

"Whoa!" screamed Grumpy, as up ahead he saw where the water dropped over the falls.

"Peep! Peep!" chirped the tiny bird.

Grumpy valiantly tried swimming upstream with one arm, but the current was too strong. All of a sudden they shot over the lip of a waterfall and *kerplunked* with a heavy splash in the pool below.

"Well," grumbled Grumpy a moment later as he dragged himself and the bird up onto the riverbank, "I suppose getting a little water-logged is better than landing on our sit-downers on the hard forest floor, eh, buster?"

"Peep! Peep!" agreed the bird.

"You can say that again!" said Grumpy.

"Peep! Peep!"

Sitting down on the bank of the river, Grumpy cradled the tiny bird in his hands as he blew the bird's fluff dry with his warm breath. When the bird was dry, Grumpy set him on his shoulder and walked back upriver to where the bird had fallen from his nest.

"Going to be a mite more suspicious this time about where I put my feet down!" he told the bird as he began climbing the tree.

"Peep! Peep!"

When Grumpy reached the nest, he peered into it cautiously and discovered that the bird had a fluff-covered brother and sister—as well as a *very* worried mother. They were all delighted when Grumpy returned the lost bird to his home.

"Peep! Peep!" chirped the nestlings and the mother bird joyously.

"Peep! Peep!" sang Grumpy's fluffy friend.

"Yeah, and peep peep to you, too," joined in Grumpy.

Before Grumpy could start his climb back down the tree, the little bird leaned over the edge of the nest and gently pecked the dwarf's nose.

"Peep! Peep!" chirped the bird gratefully.

"You're welcome, buster," scowled Grumpy, trying not to blush. "Just don't get all mushy, see? And stay in your nest!" he added, shaking his finger.

"Peep! Peep!" promised the bird.

Grumpy didn't arrive home at the cottage until well after dark. His

friends were just about to organize a search party when he limped in the door, bootless, bedraggled, and bushed.

Later, wearing dry clothes and soaking his sore feet in a tub of hot, soapy water before a roaring fire, Grumpy told the others about his adventure. While doing so, he kept a fierce scowl on his face to prevent anyone from thinking he was getting softheaded or softhearted.

But despite Grumpy's very best frowns and grumbles, the other dwarfs cheered him loudly and slapped him on the back as they told him what a great fellow he was.

And later still, when Grumpy was sitting alone by the fire, Bashful walked quietly up to him and whispered, "Thanks, Grumpy. I should have noticed before how easy it is to see that you're not grumpy all the time. In fact," he added, "you're hardly ever grumpy at all!"

Raising an eyebrow and putting on what he knew to be his most indignant look, Grumpy snorted, "Well, you have me beat. All I ever see when I look is grumpy, grumpier, grumpiest!"

Bashful chuckled the shiest of chuckles. "You're looking in the wrong place," he explained.

"What else should I be looking at besides my own mug?" Grumpy demanded, his scowl fading into a really-wanting-to-know expression.

"It has nothing to do with the look on your face," replied Bashful. "Just look at the faces of everyone around you."

Grumpy's eyes widened in wonder and his mouth dropped open in total surprise as he realized that he *wasn't* grumpy all the time. All he had to do to remind himself of this was to see the twinkling eyes and the smiles on the faces of his friends when they looked at him.

All he had to do was to remember the shining joy to be seen in the bright black eyes of a tiny bird now sleeping peacefully at his mother's side in a cozy nest high above the floor of the forest of the seven dwarfs.

Chapter Seven

Oh, Happy's Day!

All seven of the dwarfs knew it was going to be "one of those days" long before the sun even came up. During the very darkest hour of a very dark night, a fierce autumn rainstorm began to pour onto the thatch of the cottage roof. After the warm, dry months of summer, the thatch did not welcome the icy touch of the droplets and shrank together in a hopeless effort to stay out of reach.

It was no surprise, then, that the determined dollops of rain were soon sifting down through the roof and dropping gleefully onto the heads, faces, and feet of the snoring dwarfs. In fact, in very little time it appeared to be raining as hard on the inside of the cottage as it was on the outside.

"What in the name of waterlogged toe bones is going on here?" demanded Grumpy sleepily as the dwarfs gathered in one of the larger dry spots between leaks and wrung out each other's soggy nightshirts.

"Yeah," agreed Sleepy grumpily, "what are we doing up when the sun isn't?"

"It seems," chuckled Happy, spreading a blanket above the huddled dwarfs as a makeshift umbrella, "that our roof isn't any readier for the end of summer than the rest of us are."

"And that's making you happy, Happy?" asked Bashful with a shiver as a cold drop of rainwater found its way down the collar of his night-shirt.

"Well," admitted Happy with a shrug and a grin, "it could be worse."

"How?" squeaked Doc in surprise as all the dwarfs stared at Happy in amazement. "How would it be curse . . . I mean, how could it be worse?"

"Instead of getting this nice free shower from Mother Nature," Happy pointed out, "we'd have to take a *bath* . . . sooner or later."

"Ugh!" the dwarfs all responded together.

"A-chooo!" added Sneezy for good measure.

But after the dwarfs had managed to scramble into dry shirts and britches (it's difficult even for a rainstorm to wet clothes that have been wadded into tight little balls and tossed under the bed), they hurried downstairs and discovered the cottage to be in even worse shambles than usual.

There were leaks everywhere. Large puddles of water had collected on the floor, furniture was soaked and dripping, lamps and candle-holders were full of standing water, and the cottage had taken on the appearance of a large shower that someone had first stacked full of soiled plates, pots, pans, and silverware, then turned on the faucets, and finally had forgotten.

"How are we going to clean this up in the dark?" groaned Doc. "We'll have been washed away by the time the sun comes up."

"We'll simply have to have a birthday party for the cottage," laughed Happy.

"See what happens when you smile all the time?" Grumpy sniffed to the wide-eyed dwarfs. "Your thinker gets soft."

But Happy slapped Grumpy affectionately on the back and wasted no time in revealing that his thinker was as hard as ever. Pulling out bundle after carefully wrapped bundle of beeswax candles from where they'd been stored for the coming long winter nights (or for emergencies the likes of which the present moment was a perfect example), the dwarfs quickly lit the candles and set them wherever a dry spot could be found.

When the dwarfs were finished, the cottage glowed with twinkling lights as if it had been transformed into a huge candle-laden birthday cake.

"Humpf!" remarked Grumpy, who was too impressed to comment further.

"What now?" asked Bashful.

"We put the dishes and such under the leaks to catch the drips, and we sweep the water out the door!" announced Happy with a smile.

"Sounds like a lot of work," yawned Sleepy.

"It could be worse," responded Happy with another laugh.

The dwarfs exchanged another look of surprise.

"All right, Happy," sniffled Sneezy at last. "How could it be worse?"

"Instead of having to mop the floors and wash the dishes when we're *through,*" explained the broadly grinning Happy, "we'll have it all done at once!"

The dwarfs' mouths dropped open in awe, then grins spread slowly over their faces as they realized Happy was right again.

It wasn't more than a moment and they were all sweeping and mopping and setting dishes, pots, and pans beneath the leaks as they all whistled up a storm while they worked . . . even Grumpy.

And when each trickle had received its very own dish into which to drip, the standing water had been swept away, and all the furniture had been thoroughly wiped dry and carefully stacked away from the leaks, the dwarfs turned to Happy once again.

"Now what?" they wanted to know. Their beds were too wet to sleep in, the haphazardly piled furniture was impossible to sit in, and it was too dark to trudge off to work. They waited anxiously for what Happy would say this time. They were not disappointed.

"We'll have a picnic," he exclaimed.

This time no one looked at him strangely but rather they waited patiently to see exactly what he had in mind.

Unfolding a large blanket on the dry floor in front of the roaring fireplace, Happy spread out a breakfast of odds and ends retrieved from the kitchen pantry. Then, after he and the others had seated themselves and were munching contentedly, listening to the rain raining

and the leaks leaking, Happy asked, "Now, who is going to tell the first ghost story?"

"I am," said Grumpy, immediately getting into the spirit of the moment.

Much later, when Doc was in the midst of telling *his* story, the rising sun suddenly beamed through the cottage windows. The startled dwarfs looked up to see that the storm clouds had dissipated and a beautiful morning was upon them.

"Oh!" gasped Doc in a disappointed voice. "I suppose it's time to stop."

A chorus of protests resounded from the others. Dopey instantly sprang to his feet and darted around the cottage, pulling shades down

over the windows until the room was once again as cozy as midnight, illuminated only by the flickering candles and crackling fire.

"Go ahead, Doc," called out Happy. "Finish the story. Things could be worse, you know."

"That's true, Happy," agreed Doc. "But they certainly couldn't be much better."

All the other dwarfs shouted in agreement. The stories went on and on. And every single one of them ended happily ever after.

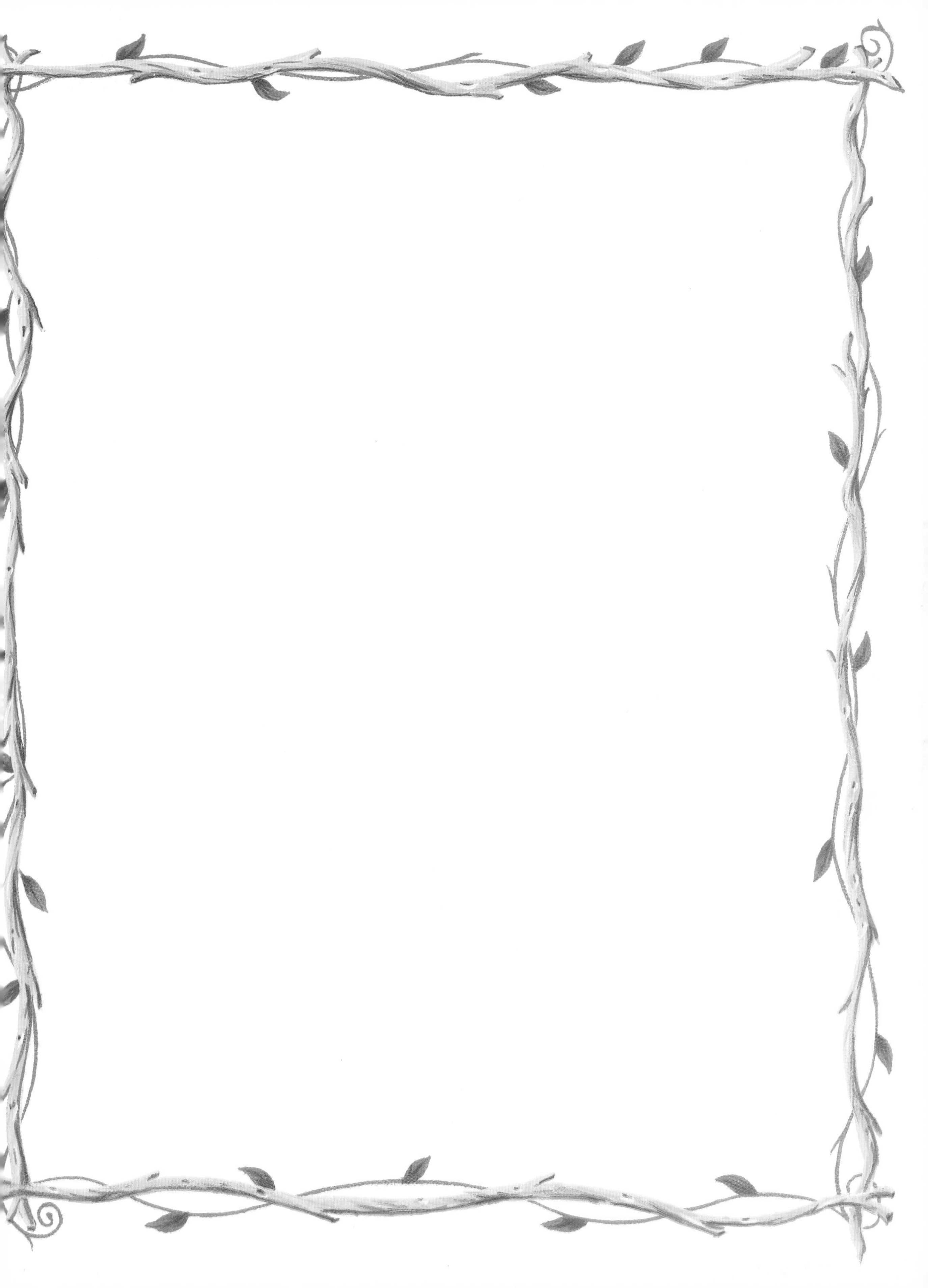